er.

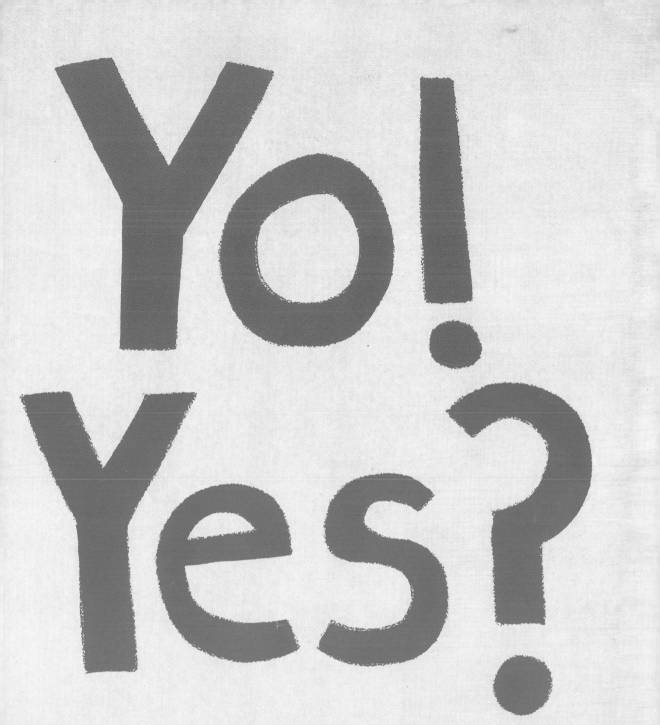

Yo! Yes?

BY

Chris Raschka

ORCHARD BOOKS NEW YORK

Orchard Books, 95 Madison Avenue, New York, NY 10016

Manufactured in the United States of America. Printed by Barton Press, Inc. Bound by Horowitz/Rae. Book design by Chris Raschka. The text of this book is hand lettered. The illustrations are watercolor and charcoal pencil, reproduced in full color.

3   4   5   6   7   8   9   10

Library of Congress Cataloging-in-Publication Data

Raschka, Christopher.

Yo! Yes? / Chris Raschka.   p.   cm. "A Richard Jackson book"—P.

Summary: Two lonely characters, one black and one white, meet on the street and become friends.

ISBN 0-531-05469-1.   ISBN 0-531-08619-4 (lib. bdg.)

[1. Friendship—Fiction.   2. Race relations—Fiction.   3. Afro-Americans—Fiction.]   I. Title.   PZ7.R18148Yo 1993

[E]—dc20   92-25644

FOR

my parents

Yes?

Who?

Yes, you.

What's up?

Not much.

Why?

No
fun.

No
friends.

Yes.

Hmmm?